DESMOND and the NAUGHTY BUGS

LINDA ASHMAN   illustrated by ANIK MCGRORY

DUTTON CHILDREN'S BOOKS

For Jackson, who taught me all about Naughtybugs.
With love—
L.A.

For my sister, Kirsten—
A.M.

Special thanks to Patrick for being a wonderful Desmond. —A.M.

DUTTON CHILDREN'S BOOKS
A division of Penguin Young Readers Group
Published by the Penguin Group • Penguin Group (USA) Inc., 375 Hudson Street, New York, New York 10014, U.S.A.
Penguin Group (Canada), 90 Eglinton Avenue East, Suite 700, Toronto, Ontario, Canada M4P 2Y3 (a division of Pearson Penguin Canada Inc.) • Penguin Books Ltd,
80 Strand, London WC2R ORL, England • Penguin Ireland, 25 St Stephen's Green, Dublin 2, Ireland (a division of Penguin Books Ltd) • Penguin Group (Australia),
250 Camberwell Road, Camberwell, Victoria 3124, Australia (a division of Pearson Australia Group Pty Ltd) • Penguin Books India Pvt Ltd, 11 Community Centre,
Panchsheel Park, New Delhi - 110 017, India • Penguin Group (NZ), Cnr Airborne and Rosedale Roads, Albany, Auckland 1310, New Zealand (a division of Pearson
New Zealand Ltd) • Penguin Books (South Africa) (Pty) Ltd, 24 Sturdee Avenue, Rosebank, Johannesburg 2196, South Africa •
Penguin Books Ltd, Registered Offices: 80 Strand, London WC2R ORL, England

Text copyright © 2006 by Linda Ashman
Illustrations copyright © 2006 by Anik Scannell McGrory

Library of Congress Cataloging-in-Publication Data

Ashman, Linda.
Desmond and the Naughtybugs / by Linda Ashman; illustrated by Anik McGrory. – 1st. ed.
p. cm.
Summary: Desmond is a well-behaved boy most of the time, but sometimes, when he is attacked by Peskies,
Sloggies, and Squirmies, he cannot seem to be good.
ISBN 0-525-47203-7
[1. Behavior—Fiction.] I. McGrory, Anik, ill. II. Title.
PZ7.A82675Des 2006
[E]—dc22 2005003283

Published in the United States by Dutton Children's Books,
a division of Penguin Young Readers Group
345 Hudson Street, New York, New York 10014
www.penguin.com/youngreaders

Designed by Irene Vandervoort
Manufactured in China   First Edition
1 3 5 7 9 10 8 6 4 2

Desmond was a sweet boy . . . usually. Most days, he hugged his mom and dad, patted his dog, Buster, and got ready for school on time.

He hardly ever left his toys on the stairway and was always willing to help fix a drippy faucet or water the gardenias.

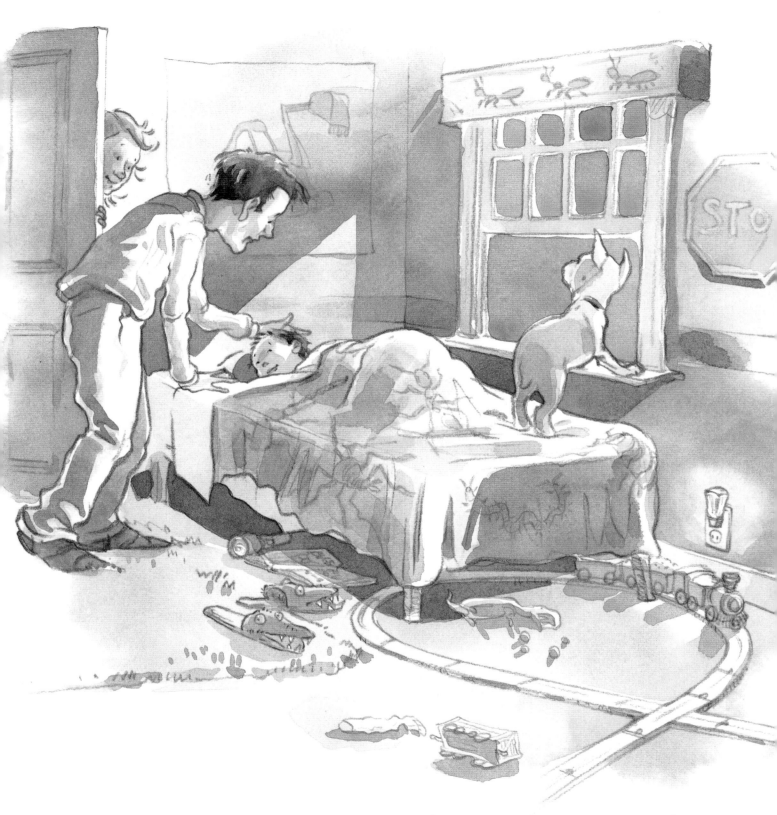

Desmond tried to be good all the time. And most of the time he was.

But when the Naughtybugs showed up, it was hard to be good. VERY hard. And you just never knew when they might show up.

On Monday, Desmond woke to find a swarm of Sloggies sprinkling him with Dawdle Dust. He got tangled in his underwear, put his overalls on backward, and crawled like a snail to breakfast.

When at last he made it to his chair, the Sloggies grabbed his spoon and played with his oatmeal, refusing to let him eat.

"The Sloggies, I see," sighed Mother. "We'll never get to school at this rate."

Desmond was slowly brushing each tooth in his mouth—for the tenth time—when his best friend, Henry, showed up with a new fire engine.

At the sound of the siren, the Sloggies vanished. Desmond flung his toothbrush in the sink and raced downstairs.

Tuesday after school, Desmond was at the market with Mother. He was choosing some bananas when he discovered a Pesky on his shoulder.

"Beg for candy," it ordered.

Desmond felt a sudden craving for licorice, but he knew what his mother would say.

"Bad idea," whispered Desmond.

He steered the shopping cart toward the melons.

"Bump that display," the Pesky directed.

"Go away," whispered Desmond.

"Pull that apple," it commanded.

Desmond eyed the stack of fruit, wondering what would happen if he removed just one tiny apple.

"Do it!" ordered the Pesky.

Desmond pulled, laughing hysterically as an avalanche of apples tumbled to the floor. The Pesky dove behind a cabbage when the store manager appeared.

Mother put Desmond in the shopping cart and passed right by the bakery without even stopping for a cookie.

Wednesday evening, Desmond and his parents were having dinner at his favorite restaurant. Desmond was explaining the difference between a backhoe and a bulldozer when all of a sudden the Squirmies showed up with their spritzers full of Fidgey Mist.

They sprayed Desmond's hands, forcing him to fiddle with his fork and fling peas with his spoon.

They sprayed more on his seat, causing him to bounce in his chair after each bite of macaroni and cheese.
"Please sit still and eat your dinner," said his father.

Desmond tried very hard to sit still. He pretended he was a statue, but having stone arms made it difficult to eat. Then he imagined he was glued to his seat, but the glue was no match for the powerful Fidgey Mist.

Desmond slid off his chair and under the table.

Just as he was crawling out, a waiter tripped over him, sending a tray full of dishes flying through the air. At the sound of the crash, the Squirmies grabbed their spritzers and sprinted across town to Henry's house.

On Thursday afternoon, a sudden downpour ruined Desmond's plans for a trip to the park. The Whineys, who thrive on rainy days, began gathering in the playroom. Finding Desmond looking mournfully out the window, they proposed another form of entertainment.

"Let's rile your mother," they suggested.
Desmond stared at the rain, trying to ignore them.
"Just a little," said the Whineys.
"She's busy," said Desmond.
"Oh, come on," they insisted. "What else is there to do?"

Desmond considered this. He picked up his fire truck but wasn't in the mood for a rescue. He stood before his easel but could only paint black clouds. He flipped through his favorite bug book, but even the spider page didn't hold his interest.

It was no use. There wasn't a single thing to do.

He followed the Whineys to his mother's office and tugged at her sleeve.

"I'm THIRRRRRRSTY," he said.

"Oh?" said Mother.

"I need AAAAAPPLE juice," said Desmond, tugging harder.

"I didn't hear the magic word," she said.

"NOWWWWW!" demanded Desmond, stomping his foot. Mother's stern look sent the Whineys scrambling for the basement.

"PLEASE," said Desmond. But it was too late. Desmond sat in his time-out chair, with no toys and no apple juice, suddenly remembering all sorts of fun things to do in the playroom.

By Friday night, the whole family was weary from the long week. Dad yawned. Mom sighed. Desmond rubbed his eyes. Conditions were perfect for a Snarly infestation. They showed up at bath time.

"Hold still!" said Father. "I need to scrub your feet."

"Scrub your own smelly feet!" said Desmond.

"Talk nice!" said Mother.

"Phooey!" snapped Desmond. The Snarlies grabbed Desmond's hand, forcing him to throw his ducky in the water.

SPLASH!!!

Lather landed on Father's head.
"No splashing!" said Father. The Snarlies grabbed Father's hand, forcing him to throw the rubber whale in the water.

SPLASH!!!

Lather landed on Mother's nose.

"No splashing!" said Mother. The Snarlies grabbed Mother's hand, forcing her to smack a chickie in the water.

SPLASH!!!

"STOP THAT, YOU LATHER-NOSE!"
yelled Desmond, splashing with both hands.

"STOP THAT, YOU FOAMY-FACE!"
yelled Mother, splashing back.

"STOP THAT, YOU BUBBLE-HEADS!"
yelled Father, splashing them both.

The soap bubbles started hatching Gigglies. The more splashing, the more Gigglies hatched. Very soon, the room was filled with them. The Snarlies can't stand the Gigglies and disappeared at the first sound of laughter.

After the bath, the three of them snuggled on the couch, reading books.

"What a week of Naughtybugs!" sighed Mother.

"I know," said Desmond.

"Thank goodness they're gone at last," said Father.

"Forever!" said Desmond.

They tucked Desmond into bed and kissed him good night. "I'll be good from now on!" he promised.

And he was . . .

mostly.

At least until the busload of Grumblies drove over from Henry's house and slipped in through the back door.

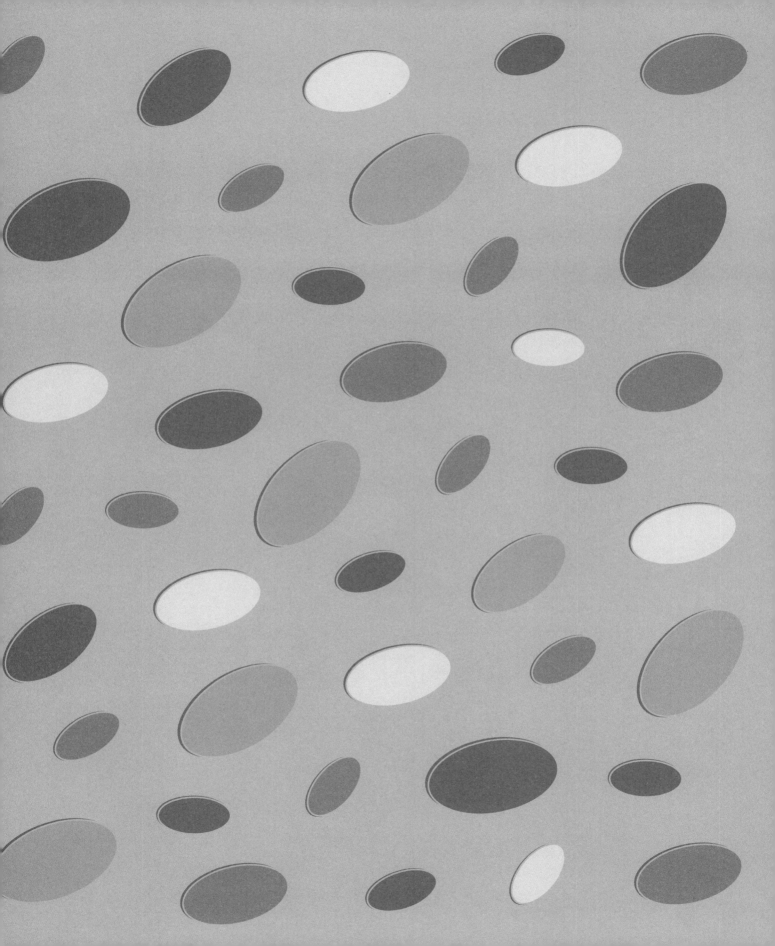